ANGEL CAT SUGAR

Spring Picnic

By Ellie O'Ryan
Illustrated by Sachiho Hino

ANGEL CAT SUGAR
characters created by Yuko Shimizu

SCHOLASTIC INC.
New York Toronto London Auckland
Sydney Mexico City New Delhi Hong Kong

ISBN: 978-0-545-16394-1

12 11 10 9 8 7 6 5 4 3 2   10 11 12 13 14/0

Printed in the U.S.A.   40
First printing, January 2010

The sun is shining.
The flowers are blooming.
It's a beautiful spring day!

Sugar has an idea!
She will make a picnic
to share with her friends.

Sugar gets the picnic basket.
Then she gets the picnic blanket.

Next Sugar makes sandwiches and cupcakes.

Sugar packs the picnic basket.
Then she calls her friends and
asks them to come over.

Look!
Here come Basil, Parsley, and Thyme.

Sugar can't wait to tell them
about the picnic she made.

But first, Parsley says,
"What a great day!
I brought kites for us to fly!"

"I want to find out
which kite will fly higher.
The circle? The heart?
The triangle? Or the diamond?"

Basil says, "We can fly kites another day.
Let's go to the cherry grove
and look at the new cherry blossoms!"

Thyme says, "But I want to play
hide-and-seek! Hide-and-seek is the best!"

Sugar wants everyone to have fun.
But all her friends want to do
something different.

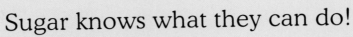

Sugar knows what they can do!

"I have an idea!" she says.
"Let's walk to the top of Misty Mountain first."

"Look, Basil," says Sugar.
"There are cherry blossoms!"

"They are so pretty!" cries Basil.

Next the friends walk past a field.
Sugar sees the grass sway
in the breeze.

"Parsley, this is a perfect place
to fly kites!" she says.

Parsley gives everybody a kite.
The wind carries the kites
up into the sky.

Parsley says, "Wow! The diamond kite
flies higher than the other kites!"

Next the friends walk through the woods.

"What a good place to play
hide-and-seek!" says Sugar.

Even the squirrels want to play!
Thyme counts to ten.
"Ready or not, here I come!" he calls.

After Thyme finds his friends,
he rubs his tummy.
"I'm hungry!" he says.

Basil and Parsley say, "So are we!"
Sugar smiles and says, "Follow me!"

At the top of Misty Mountain,
Sugar shares her surprise.
"I made a yummy picnic to share!"

It's a delicious end to a spring day!

Dear Family and Friends of New Readers,

Welcome to Scholastic Reader. We have taken more than eighty years of experience with teachers, parents, and children and put it into a program that is designed to match your child's interest and skills. Each Scholastic Reader is designed to support your child's efforts to learn how to read at every age and every stage.

- First Reader
- Preschool - Kindergarten
- ABC's
- First words

- Beginning Reader
- Preschool - Grade 1
- Sight words
- Words to sound out
- Simple sentences

- Developing Reader
- Grades 1 – 2
- New vocabulary
- Longer sentences

- Growing Reader
- Grades 1 – 3
- Reading for inspiration and information

On the back of every book, we have indicated the grade level, guided reading level, Lexile® level, and word count. You can use this information to find a book that is a good fit for your child.

For ideas about sharing books with your new reader, please visit www.scholastic.com. Enjoy helping your child learn to read and love to read!

Happy Reading!

—Francie Alexander
Chief Academic Officer
Scholastic Inc.

How will Sugar and her friends spend a sunny day?

LEVEL PRE 1 — FIRST READER · 30-100 WORDS
ABC's & first words.

LEVEL 1 — BEGINNING READER · 50-250 WORDS
Sight words, words to sound out & simple sentences.

LEVEL 2 — DEVELOPING READER · 250-750 WORDS
New vocabulary & longer sentences.

LEVEL 3 — GROWING READER · 700-1500 WORDS
Reading for inspiration & information.

Based on the best research about how children learn to read, Scholastic Readers are developed under the supervision of reading experts and are educator approved.

DEVELOPING READER	GRADE LEVEL	GUIDED READING LEVEL	LEXILE® LEVEL	WORD COUNT
Level 2	1-2	I	410L	340

"Scholastic Readers are designed to support your child's efforts to learn how to read at every age and every stage. Enjoy helping your child learn to read and love to read."
— Francie Alexander
CHIEF ACADEMIC OFFICER
SCHOLASTIC INC.

© 2010 YUKO SHIMIZU/TACT.C.INC.

$3.99 US/$4.99 CAN

ISBN: 978-0-545-16394-1

50399

9 780545 163941

SCHOLASTIC

www.scholastic.com

ACCOUNTING

AN INTERNATIONAL PERSPECTIVE

FOURTH EDITION

MUELLER

GERNON

MEEK